Disney · PIXAR

THE WORLD OF

Cars

Race Team

By Dennis R. Shealy

Illustrated by the Disney Storybook Artists

Random House 🏠 New York

Lightning McQueen
is going to a race.

Dear Parent:

Congratulations! Your child is taking the first steps on an exciting journey. The destination? Independent reading!

STEP INTO READING® will help your child get there. The program offers five steps to reading success. Each step includes fun stories and colorful art. There are also Step into Reading Sticker Books, Step into Reading Math Readers, Step into Reading Write-In Readers, Step into Reading Phonics Readers, and Step into Reading Phonics First Steps! Boxed Sets—a complete literacy program with something for every child.

Learning to Read, Step by Step!

Ready to Read Preschool–Kindergarten
• big type and easy words • rhyme and rhythm • picture clues
For children who know the alphabet and are eager to begin reading.

Reading with Help Preschool–Grade 1
• basic vocabulary • short sentences • simple stories
For children who recognize familiar words and sound out new words with help.

Reading on Your Own Grades 1–3
• engaging characters • easy-to-follow plots • popular topics
For children who are ready to read on their own.

Reading Paragraphs Grades 2–3
• challenging vocabulary • short paragraphs • exciting stories
For newly independent readers who read simple sentences with confidence.

Ready for Chapters Grades 2–4
• chapters • longer paragraphs • full-color art
For children who want to take the plunge into chapter books but still like colorful pictures.

STEP INTO READING® is designed to give every child a successful reading experience. The grade levels are only guides. Children can progress through the steps at their own speed, developing confidence in their reading, no matter what their grade.

Remember, a lifetime love of reading starts with a single step!

For Sis

Visit us on the Web!

www.stepintoreading.com
www.randomhouse.com/kids/disney

Educators and librarians, for a variety of teaching tools, visit us at
www.randomhouse.com/teachers

Library of Congress Cataloging-in-Publication Data
Shealy, Dennis R.
    Race team / by Dennis R. Shealy; illustrated by the Disney Storybook Artists.
    p. cm.
ISBN 978-0-7364-2571-1
ISBN 978-0-7364-8065-9 (gibraltar library binding)
I. Disney Storybook Artists. II. Cars (Motion picture) III. Title.
PZ7.S53767Rac 2008
[E]–dc22
2008009106

Printed in the United States of America   10 9 8 7 6 5 4 3   First Edition

Mack will take him.

All the cars get ready.

Sarge and Flo bring
cans of gas and oil.

Guido loads Fillmore
with water for McQueen.

Guido packs spare tires.

Mater drives in circles.

He is excited!

The cars drive
to the race.
It is far.

Poor Guido gets tired.

Mater gives him a tow.

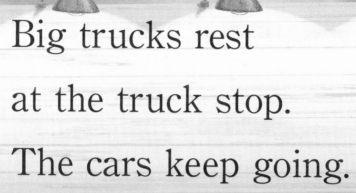

Big trucks rest
at the truck stop.
The cars keep going.

Mater sees
McQueen and Mack.
There are cars
all around them.

Reporters ask McQueen
about the race.
They take many pictures.

The racetrack is a
busy place!
Mack parks in the pit.

He watches McQueen
practice.

Doc puts on his headset.

It is time for the race.

Mater cheers.

He wants McQueen

to win!

The pit crew is ready.

McQueen drives
to the starting line.
His pit crew yells,
"Go, McQueen, go!"

51 FABULOUS HUDSON HORNET

The race starts. <u>Vroom!</u>

McQueen is in front!

He drives the fastest.

McQueen gets tired.

But he keeps going.

Lightning McQueen
wins the race!
Ka-chow!

The race is over.
McQueen and Mack
head home!